Seed Man

aiko ikegami

PUBLISHED BY SLEEPING BEAR PRESS

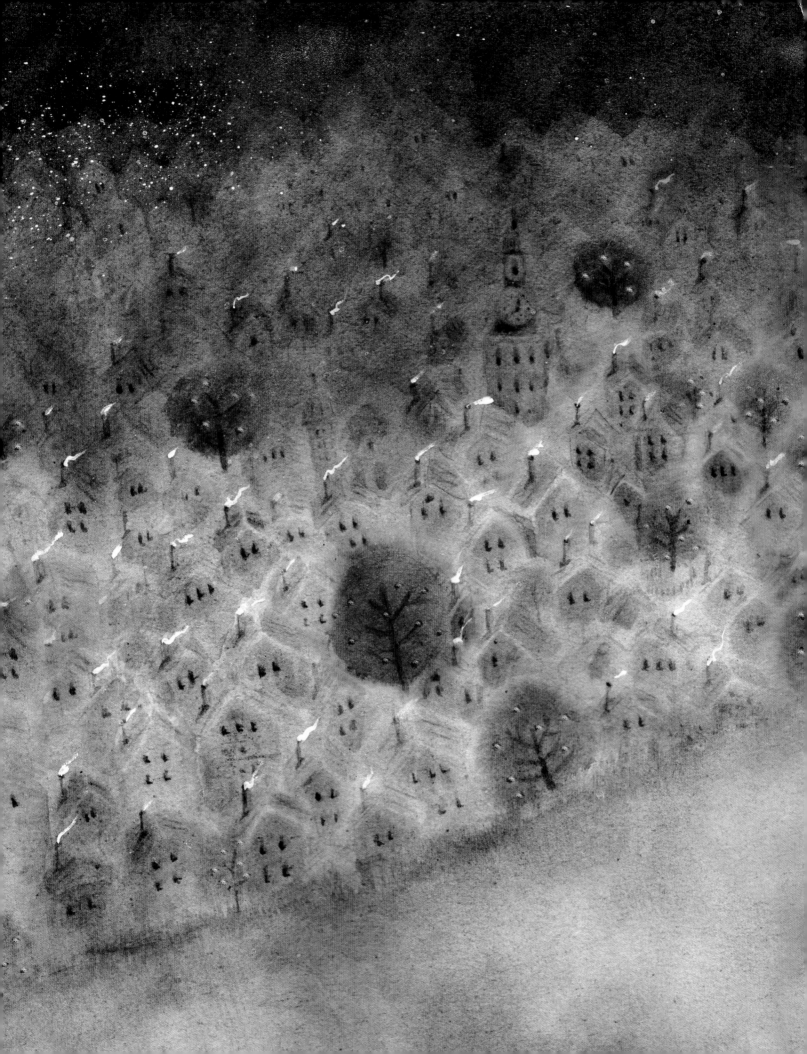

One day Seed Man came to town.

He planted a seed

and called the fairies.

The fairies took
good care of the seed.

It grew into a seedling.

The seedling grew into a tree.

The tree bore special fruit.

The fairies delivered
Seed Man's gifts
all over town.

Even if someone didn't know he needed a gift,

Seed Man and
the fairies knew.

"I don't want a dog,"
said the man.

"Ay yi yi."

Things began to go well.

But then . . .

The man looked at the
broken picture.

The man wondered where the
dog would go in the rain.

He went to look.

But he didn't find the dog.

The fairies did.

And Seed Man knew it was time, and told the fairies.

The fairies brought the seeds.

One day Seed Man came to town.

For my father, Morihiro Tokuni (1936–2016).

I love you.

— Aiko

My many sincere thanks to Anna Olswanger, Barb McNally, Jennifer Bacheller,

and Sleeping Bear Press for helping me to make this book.